THE HUTCHINSON BOOK OF
SCHOOL STORIES

HUTCHINSON

London Sydney Auckland Johannesburg

THE HUTCHINSON BOOK OF SCHOOL STORIES
A HUTCHINSON BOOK 0 091 89362 3

Published in Great Britain by Hutchinson,
an imprint of Random House Children's Books

This edition published 2004

1 3 5 7 9 10 8 6 4 2

RANDOM HOUSE CHILDREN'S BOOKS
61–63 Uxbridge Road, London W5 5SA
A division of The Random House Group Ltd

RANDOM HOUSE AUSTRALIA (PTY) LTD
20 Alfred Street, Milsons Point, Sydney,
New South Wales 2061, Australia

RANDOM HOUSE NEW ZEALAND LTD
18 Poland Road, Glenfield, Auckland 10, New Zealand

RANDOM HOUSE (PTY) LTD
Endulini, 5A Jubilee Road, Parktown 2193, South Africa

THE RANDOM HOUSE GROUP Limited Reg. No. 954009
www.kidsatrandomhouse.co.uk

A CIP catalogue record for this book is available from the British Library.

Book design by Dicki Dot Ltd

Printed in China

CONTENTS

BAD BORIS GOES TO SCHOOL

Susie Jenkin-Pearce

"BORIS," said Maisie one morning,
"you're old enough to go to school."

"School!" gasped Boris. "No I'm not. I hate school!"

"Nonsense," said Maisie.
"You'll do painting and writing.
You'll learn to read and play lots
of games. You'll love it!"

"No I won't," growled Boris.

"Wish I could go," said
the kitten.

But Boris just flattened his
ears and refused to listen.

The next day, they all went out to buy Boris's school things.

They bought pencils,

a pack of felt-tip pens,

a painting
apron,

and a lunch box.

Boris didn't even say thank
you. "I hate school," was all
he said.

But all young elephants must go to school and soon it was Boris's first day.

The classroom was full of excited animals saying hello to their friends from last term, and there were some new animals looking a bit scared.

"This is Boris," said Maisie to Mrs Prism, the teacher.

When the grown-ups had gone, Mrs Prism called the noisy animals together. "Hush, now," she said. "You're as noisy as a class full of children."

Boris found himself next to a small crocodile who couldn't stop crying. "Don't cry," he said. "I'll look after you."

The morning went very quickly. They did painting, then music and movement.

First they pretended to be fire-breathing dragons. Then Mrs Prism let them choose something for themselves.

"I'm a tree," cried Boris, "swaying in the breeze."

At lunchtime, Boris and the
crocodile shared their sandwiches.
The crocodile ate one of Boris's
buns. She was already feeling a
lot happier.

In the afternoon they played with sand and . . . water.

Mrs Prism seemed very pleased with Boris. His trunk
was just right for clearing up outside . . .

. . . and for collecting pencils.

"Boris!" said Mrs Prism. "I
don't know how I managed
without you."

Back at home Maisie was having a lovely time playing school with the kitten when she suddenly looked at her watch.

"Goodness me!" she cried. "It's time to collect Boris. Someone who hates school won't like to be kept waiting."

But when Maisie and the kitten arrived, instead of
an elephant who hated school, there was a proud,
smiling elephant who didn't even notice them at first.
"Well," said Maisie, "how do you like school?"

But Boris wasn't even listening.
He was too busy showing
the kitten how he could
turn into a tree.

RUBY TO THE RESCUE

Maggie Glen

TODAY'S THE day, thought Ruby.
I can't wait to see what school is like . . .

Ruby had heard a lot about school, and at last she was going to see for herself. Mum waved goodbye, and Ruby and Susie set off with Grandfather.

At school, Susie left Ruby in the playhouse while she listened to the teacher. The other toys stared at Ruby and pointed.

"You're funny looking," said a big bear with a torn ear.

"I'm Ruby and I'm special," said Ruby firmly. "Who are you?"

"We're Anyone's bears," said the big bear, putting his arm around a small bear.

"Anyone's bears?" said Ruby.

Suddenly, the door of the playhouse opened and in rushed two children. They both grabbed the big ragged bear.

"It's mine!" shouted the boy.

"No, it's mine!" shrieked the girl. "I saw him first."

They tugged and tore at the big bear. Ruby growled but they didn't hear.

"Stop this at once," said the teacher, looking into the playhouse. "They're anyone's bears. You have to share them. No wonder the toys get into such a state!"

"Phew! That was nasty," said the ragged bear, when the children had gone.

"You've got another hole," said the small bear.

"And I thought school was supposed to be fun," Ruby muttered.

Just then they heard the teacher.

"I see the toys have become very dirty again. Shall we give them a wash, children?"

"Oh no!" said the big ragged bear. "That's the very worst thing that can happen."

"I was soggy for a week last time," said the small bear.

"Quick, under here," whispered Ruby as they heard the children coming towards the playhouse. Anyone's bears and Ruby dived under an old curtain in the dressing-up box.

Ruby and Anyone's bears didn't make a sound while the children collected the other toys for washing.

"I can't stand much more soapy water, or any more holes," groaned the big ragged bear. "Whatever are we going to do?"

"Well, it's no good staying here where the children don't look after you properly," said Ruby. "You need to be with someone who thinks you're special."

"Us? Special?" said the small bear.

"All bears are special," replied Ruby.

"Don't be silly," said the ragged bear gruffly. "We're so dirty and full of holes, who would want us?"

"Of course someone will. Just let me think," said Ruby.

"I've got it," she said suddenly.

"Got what?" asked Anyone's bears.

"An idea," said Ruby. "Follow me."

While the children were busy, the three bears crept out of the room, tiptoed down the corridor, then ran right out of the school door as fast as they could.

When they reached the dustbins in the yard, Ruby stopped.

"Wait here," she said, "and I'm sure my plan will work."

Then she said goodbye and ran back inside.

The two bears looked at each other.

"We're on our own now," whispered the big bear. "I hope she's got it right."

Anyone's bears waited and waited. Suddenly they heard loud
banging noises.

"I'm scared and I'm not very big," whispered the small bear.

"I'll look after you," said the ragged bear.

Suddenly, a big deep voice boomed: "Look at these little fellas,
Tom. They look like they've had a hard time."

"Yes, they're about ready for the dustcart," said another loud
voice. "Pick 'em up, Bill."

Bill lifted Anyone's bears gently. Then the dustmen began
to smile.

"Looks like this one needs a plaster," said Tom, pointing to the big bear.

"I think they like us," whispered the small bear.

Tom laughed: "This little chap's got a squeak."

Bill put Anyone's bears carefully in the cab. "From now on you ride with us," he said.

A whole week went by. At last it was dustbin day again. Ruby watched from Susie's bedroom window. She crossed her paws and hoped her plan had worked.

At last the dustcart drew up outside Ruby's house. And there, right in the front of the cab, sat Anyone's bears.

Ruby jumped up and down and called out, "Hello, there!" They looked up and saw her waving.

"Hey, Ruby, look at me," cried the big ragged bear. "I'm special now."

"Me too!" shouted the little bear proudly.

Ruby grinned at the two happy bears. "Of course you're special," she said. "Just like me."

RABBIT GETS READY

Claire Fletcher

RABBIT WOKE up feeling different. Today was a very special day – his first day at a new school. He was excited and happy, but he was nervous too and there was a strange feeling in his tummy. It was eight o'clock. He had to get dressed quickly if he was going to be there on time. He didn't want to walk in late with everyone looking at him – Rabbit felt quite weak at the thought.

He opened his wardrobe. He had lots of clothes: coats and trousers and shoes, and shirts and jumpers. What should he put on?

Everyone else will know what to wear, thought Rabbit. It was so unfair.

He tried on his knitted swimming costume. It was great for diving and somersaulting at the pool, but not quite right for school.

Next Rabbit put on a striped jacket and a straw hat. He had spent a lovely day with Dog on the river bank eating peanut butter sandwiches and looking at the boats. Maybe . . . The jacket was smart enough, but the others were sure to laugh at him if he wore that hat.

What about his beloved dungarees, with safety pins
where the buttons should have been? He usually wore them
chug-chugging along on board the big red tractor at the
farm. But Rabbit threw them on the floor. Everyone would
think he was a real scruff in those.

Rabbit's funny feeling was growing. All he wanted was to
fit in. It was such an important day, but he just couldn't seem
to make up his mind.

He unruffled his best hat, trimmed with feathers. It had been such a hit at Monkey's party. But no, thought Rabbit. He didn't want to draw quite that much attention to himself. Not on his first day anyway.

Rabbit frantically rummaged about. Something big and bright caught his eye. It was the jumper Aunt Maud had given him last summer. "I expect I shall be quite warm enough without that!" said Rabbit, scornfully.

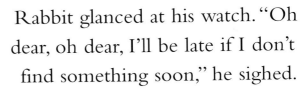

Rabbit glanced at his watch. "Oh dear, oh dear, I'll be late if I don't find something soon," he sighed.

He spotted his blue sailor suit and tried it on. As he marched up and down with a nautical air he could almost taste the salt and hear the call of the seagulls.

Rabbit was beginning to wish that he could run away to sea. As far as he knew, sailors didn't go to school.

Poor Rabbit. Suddenly he heard the *beep beep* of the school bus outside the door. There was no time to lose. Rabbit grabbed the last thing from his cupboard – his stripy football jersey. He ran out of the door as fast as he could, clutching his lunch box in his paws.

The school yard brimmed with all the colours of the rainbow. A group of pigs were having a picnic in the middle. There was a water trough with boats and ships and there was even a tortoise

on a big red tractor. Rabbit wanted to join in, but the funny
feeling in his tummy was worse.

He felt very alone and just a little bit scared.

Then he saw a small bear standing timidly in the corner of the playground. He did look smart, but he didn't look very happy.

Rabbit took a deep breath, marched over and took the bear by the paw. "Are you new?" said Rabbit. The bear nodded, shyly. Rabbit smiled. "Come on then," he said.

Together they ran as fast as they could to the end of the
playground. "Kick it here . . ." "To me . . ." came the cries
from all around. Rabbit jumped for joy – he would soon make
friends. And his funny feeling had quite, quite gone. Perhaps
tomorrow he would wear . . . Oh bother, thought Rabbit.
Who cares . . . ? And he let out a shout – "Let's PLAY!"

UNICORN DREAMS

Dyan Sheldon and Neil Reed

THE FIRST time Dan saw the unicorn, he was
staring out of the window of his classroom
watching the traffic below. He saw a long white
tail, plaited with a coloured ribbon, vanish
behind a van.

Dan's teacher rapped on her desk. "Dan,"
she said. "Dan, are you daydreaming again?"

Dan looked up. "No, miss," he said.

Dan's teacher smiled. "Then perhaps you'd like to tell the class what you were looking at that was more interesting than our lesson."

Dan pointed to the window. "There's a unicorn outside," he told her.

Dan's teacher didn't look out of the window. She stopped smiling. "A unicorn? You saw a unicorn in front of the school?"

"That's right," said Dan, nodding with excitement. "It has a

long white tail, tied with a coloured ribbon."

The other children began to laugh. "Dreamy Dan," they shouted. "He sees unicorns in Lupton Road."

Dan bent his head over his sums.

The second time Dan saw the unicorn, he was sitting on the school bus with his class.

The unicorn was gazing from the window of the video store.

It shook its head when it saw Dan.

Dan waved back.

Dan's teacher appeared at his shoulder. "Who are you waving at, Dan?" she asked.

"The unicorn," cried Dan, pointing towards the video store. "It shook its head at me."

Dan's teacher didn't look back at the video store. She squeezed her lips together. "The unicorn," she repeated. "The unicorn was in the video shop?"

"Dreamy Dan! Dreamy Dan!" chanted the other children. "He thinks unicorns go shopping in the high street."

Even the bus driver started to laugh.

The third time Dan saw the unicorn, he was sitting under a tree in the school yard while the children played their games.

The unicorn was on the other side of the playground, eating an apple it had found in the bin. When it saw Dan, the unicorn threw the apple in the air and caught it on its horn.

Dan's teacher blew her whistle. "Dan! Why aren't you playing with everyone else? What are you doing?"

"I'm watching the unicorn," Dan called back. He raised his hand. "It's over there."

Dan's teacher didn't turn round. "A unicorn in the playground?" she said sourly.

"That's right!" cried Dan. "It's juggling an apple."

The other children had stopped their games and were all watching Dan.

"Dreamy Dan! Dreamy Dan!" they yelled. "He thinks unicorns come from the circus."

Dan's teacher blew her whistle again, but no one heard it because they were laughing too much.

When Dan got home from school that afternoon, the unicorn was lying in the forecourt in a pool of grass. It stood up when it saw Dan.

The bells in its mane jangled as it followed him into the lift. "You can't come in," said Dan. But the unicorn went in anyway.

Dan and the unicorn got out on the thirteenth floor. "You can't come in," Dan told the unicorn as he opened the door to his flat. "Everyone says you aren't real." But the unicorn went in anyway.

All afternoon, Dan waited for the unicorn to vanish, but instead it followed him everywhere he went.

It shared his tea.

It helped him with his homework.

It watched television with him.

When Dan went to bed, the unicorn went too.
They had wonderful dreams.

The next day, the unicorn walked to school with Dan.
When Dan went to school on his own he walked through
ordinary streets, past ordinary buildings.

But when the unicorn went with him, they walked through an enchanted forest where dragons played and wizards worked spells.

They had just come to the edge of the forest when the school bell rang.

Dan was saying goodbye to the unicorn when his teacher called him in. Dan ran towards the school.

"Come on, Dreamy Dan!" yelled a boy from his class.

"Where's your unicorn?" teased another.

Dan looked back. The unicorn was gone.

Dan spent the morning staring out of the window at the dull, grey street. He missed the unicorn.

In the afternoon, it was story time. "Would anyone
like to tell a story today?" asked the teacher.
Dan raised his hand.
Everyone listened as Dan told the class how
the unicorn had followed him
into the lift.

He told them how the bells in its mane jangled and how butterflies danced in the air all around it.

He told them about their wonderful dreams. No one laughed.

"I can hear them!" shouted one of the children. "I can hear the bells!"

"Look!" cried another. "Look over there."

Suddenly, all the children could see Dan's unicorn. It stood at the top of a narrow path, leading to a forest below. It looked at Dan and flicked its tail.

This time, Dan followed the unicorn . . . and the rest of the class followed Dan.

THE LONG, BLUE BLAZER

Jeanne Willis and Susan Varley

WHEN I was five, there was a boy in my class who wore a long, blue blazer. He had short arms and short legs and big feet that stuck out from under his long, blue blazer.

He arrived one winter's day. He wandered into the classroom covered in snow and shook hands with the teacher.

She said, "You must be Wilson, the new boy."

She told him to hang up his things. He took off his cap and his scarf and his mittens. But he wouldn't take off his long, blue blazer.

The teacher asked him to, but he said he was cold, so she let him keep it on. Later on we did some painting. We all had to put plastic aprons on, but Wilson put his apron on over his long, blue blazer.

I painted my mum in a pink, flowery dress and Mary painted her mum in green, stripy trousers. But Wilson painted his mum in a long, blue blazer.

He ate his school dinner in his long, blue blazer. He did his sums in his long, blue blazer. He even did PE in his long, blue blazer.

The teacher asked him to take it off, but he said his mother would be angry if he did so she let him keep it on.

When it was time to go home, my mum came to fetch me, but nobody came for Wilson. He stood alone in his long, blue blazer, staring up at the sky. The teacher asked him why his mother hadn't come to fetch him. He said she lived too far away.

69

Wilson walked slowly through the school gates, his long, blue blazer dragging in the snow.

The teacher spoke to my mum and I was told to run after Wilson and invite him for tea.

That seemed to make him happy. But when my mum asked him to take off his long, blue blazer, he looked as if he was about to cry, so she let him keep it on.

She gave him some steak and kidney pie and sat him on her lap. He put his arms round her and started to cry. He said he was tired.

Mum carried Wilson up to my
bedroom and sat him on a chair while
she fetched him some pyjamas. When
she came back, he'd climbed into my
bunk bed in his long, blue blazer and
pulled the blankets around him. I slept
on the bottom bunk.

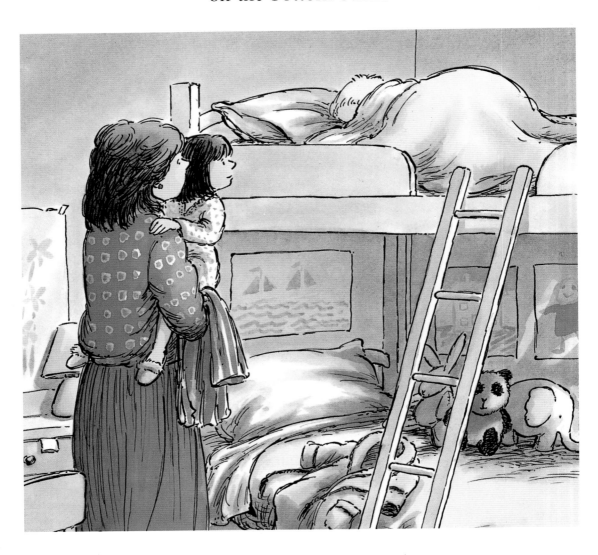

Later that night, a loud humming noise woke me up. The wind was making the curtains flap, so I got up to shut the window. I saw green and yellow flashing lights, and there, standing on the windowsill, was Wilson. Suddenly . . . he jumped.

The last I ever saw of him was his long, blue TAIL!

LEAVING MRS ELLIS

Catherine Robinson and Sue Broadley

MRS ELLIS was the nicest teacher at Leo's school. She was a kind, gentle lady with a very soft lap. Leo had been in Mrs Ellis's class for a year, but it felt as if he had known her for ever. She was so familiar to Leo, she seemed like part of the family. Not his mum: there was nobody like Mum. But very close. A big sister, maybe. Or an auntie.

Leo often thought he would like to marry Mrs Ellis when he grew up, although deep down he knew he couldn't because she was already married, to Mr Ellis. But he was very fond of her.

Every summer, before the children went off for their holidays, there was a Summer Fair. This year Leo's mum was in charge of the cake stall, and she had been busy baking cakes and freezing them for weeks.

One day when Leo got home, Mum had all the cakes laid out on the kitchen table. She was icing them, and decorating them; some with tiny coloured sweets, some with hundreds-and-thousands, some with cherries and little silver balls.

Leo's mouth watered. "Yummy," he said.

"I thought you could take this one to school tomorrow," Mum said. "I thought you could give it to Mrs Ellis."

Leo was puzzled. "Why?" he said. "I thought all the cakes were for the Summer Fair."

"It's a way of saying thank you," Mum explained.

Leo was even more puzzled and a bit worried. "Thank you for what?" he asked.

"Well," said Mum. "Thank you for having you in her class this year. Thank you for teaching you so much. Thank you for looking after you. Now, how about testing some of this shortbread?"

But Leo didn't want any shortbread. Suddenly, the cakes didn't look and smell so nice. He didn't want his tea either; he just picked at it. And later, when he went to bed, he couldn't get to sleep.

The next morning, Leo didn't want to get up.

"I want to stay in bed," he told Mum. "I'm poorly. I've got a tummy ache."

Mum felt his forehead, and looked at him. "Is it a real tummy ache?" she asked him gently. "Or an I-don't-want-to-go-to-school tummy ache?"

Leo went red, and turned away and looked at the wall.

"It's real," he whispered. "I feel sick."

"Leo," said Mum. "Tell me what's wrong."

Leo turned back again and looked at her. "It's Mrs Ellis," he said at last. "I shan't be in her class any more. Next year, somebody else will be my teacher."

"But you already knew that," Mum said. "Didn't you?"

"I knew in my head," said Leo. "I think I did. But it was only yesterday – when you made the cake – that I knew in my tummy. I don't want to leave Mrs Ellis, Mum. I want to stay in her class!"

Mum stroked his hair, and told him that he was growing up, and when you grow up things have to change; otherwise you would stay a baby for ever, and that wouldn't be right.

Leo started to feel a little better. He got up and got dressed, and went to school. But when he was running around the playground with his friend Andrew at playtime, he suddenly thought of something that made him feel ill again. He suddenly remembered who was going to be his teacher next year. It was Miss Lyons.

Everyone was scared of Miss Lyons. All the children at Leo's school were terrified of her. Even some of the teachers seemed frightened by her tallness and her stern face and her loud booming voice. Leo sometimes thought that even the parents must be scared of her.

Miss Lyons's class was always the quietest in the school; Leo thought they must be too scared to make any noise at all. And now he was to be in her class! Leo couldn't bear it.

That night, he had a terrible nightmare. He dreamed he was being chased by an enormous lion with wings like a dragon and a tail like a snake. It was coming for him, nearer and nearer and nearer . . . He woke up with a jump, hot and sweaty and with a thumping heart. Mum was bending over him, tying up her dressing gown.

"Are you all right?" she said. "You were calling Mrs Ellis. Was it a bad dream?"

Leo nodded and sat up, wiping the tears from his cheeks. "It wasn't Mrs Ellis, though," he told Mum. "It was Miss Lyons."

But he wouldn't tell her any more. It seemed so silly, now he was awake. Miss Lyons was just a lady, not a wild animal at all. She couldn't eat him, not really. Could she?

At last it was the Summer Fair. Leo had mostly been looking forward to it; it was fun, with lots of stalls to spend pocket money, and Throwing the Wet Sponge at teachers, and parents cooking beefburgers, and a Fancy Dress Parade. But part of him was sad too, because after the Summer Fair came the holidays and after the holidays there would be no more Mrs Ellis.

Mrs Ellis went to the cake stall to thank Leo's mum for the chocolate cake. Leo was there too, helping out and eating all the broken bits.

"It was delicious," said Mrs Ellis. "A wonderful cake. It was very kind of you."

"Well," said Mum, "it was from Leo, really. To say thank you."

Mrs Ellis smiled. "He's a good boy," she said. "I get very fond of all my children. I miss them all once they've moved up. And I shall miss Leo especially. He paints such good pictures. He painted a lovely picture of a lion last week; it was so good I put it up on display, on the classroom wall. He has a very vivid imagination."

Leo had heard about vivid imaginations before, from Mum. They were what gave you good ideas for paintings and stories, she said. They were what gave you terrible nightmares, about lions with dragons' wings and snakes' tails . . . On the whole, Leo wished his imagination wasn't quite so vivid.

Soon it was all over. The whole Mrs Ellis year, gone for ever. Leo was very sad to think she would never be his teacher again.

"I know it's sad," Mum told him, "but you'll soon get used to it, once you're back at school. Just as you'll soon get used to your new teacher."

"No I won't," said Leo gloomily. "It's Miss Lyons."

He tried to explain to Mum how horrible and frightening and booming Miss Lyons was, but Mum couldn't seem to understand. All she would say was, "Try not to worry. I'm sure you'll soon get to like her."

That night, Leo had the lion-dragon dream again. It was even worse than usual. Afterwards, when Mum had soothed the fear away and gone back to bed, Leo lay awake in the dark. He wondered if he would ever get over leaving Mrs Ellis.

One morning, Mum took Leo shopping with her. She had to go to the supermarket, which Leo usually hated, but Mum had promised to take him out to lunch afterwards for a treat.

"Can it be a pizza?" Leo asked her.

"It can be anything you like," Mum told him.

So he followed her around the enormous shop, and looked without interest at packets of biscuits and tins of soup while she filled the trolley. He soon realized that Mum had stopped and was talking to somebody. It wasn't until he got up close that he saw, to his horror, that the somebody was Miss Lyons. He couldn't turn and run; she'd already seen him.

"Why hello, Leo," she boomed. "And how are you today?"

Leo didn't answer. He wasn't being rude; he just couldn't speak.

Mum carried on talking to her instead, about Miss Lyons's cats, and while they talked Leo sneaked a look in Miss Lyons's wire basket. Sure enough, there were a lot of tins of cat food. There was also one frozen pork chop, two apples in a plastic bag, and a small jar of coffee. Leo looked at his mother's trolley, and all the food for Mum and Dad and him. He felt a little pang of pity for Miss Lyons and her single pork chop, and just her cats for company.

Miss Lyons was talking to him. "You paint lovely pictures, don't you, Leo?" she was saying. "I saw your lion painting on Mrs Ellis's classroom wall. Will you paint one for me? Just for fun. Just for me to enjoy. Would you do that for me?"

Leo and Mum looked at each other. Then he looked at Miss Lyons. "Yes," he said, in a loud clear voice, "Yes, I will."

He started the painting as soon as he got home, but it still took a long time to get it right. It was going to be a picture of cats, as Miss Lyons liked cats, but it didn't turn out like that.

It was a picture of his nightmare, the lion-dragon one, but in the picture Leo wasn't running away. In the picture Leo was one of King Arthur's knights, and he was standing over the lion-dragon with his sword held high in the air, because he had fought the monster and killed it, stone dead.

It was a very good painting. Leo thought it was one of the best he had ever done. "Can we take it to Miss Lyons's house?" he asked Mum, when the painting was dry.

Mum thought about it. "I think she'd like that," she said. "But we should telephone first. Are you sure you wouldn't rather post it?" Miss Lyons had given Mum her address at the supermarket.

"No," said Leo. "I want to take it to her."

So Leo and Mum took the painting round to Miss Lyons's house, which wasn't a house at all but a flat. It was a very nice flat. Leo and Mum sat down while Miss Lyons spread the painting out on her big table, and looked at it very carefully. Leo could hear the slow, gentle tick of a clock.

One of Miss Lyons's cats jumped up into Leo's lap and spread itself out, purring and pushing at him with its paws. At last Miss Lyons finished looking at the painting. She took off her glasses.

"It's very good," she said. It was funny, but she didn't seem to be quite so booming any more.

"In fact, it's excellent. And you did it all by yourself?"

Leo nodded. "It took ages," he said and explained the story of the painting, about the knight and the lion-dragon.

Miss Lyons listened carefully to Leo, and when he finished she smiled at him.

Leo had never seen Miss Lyons smile before. It changed her whole face.

"You know," she said thoughtfully, "most people would have run away from that monster. It was very brave of you to face up to it."

"I know," said Leo. "I know that, now."

"And now," said Miss Lyons, "how about some tea?"

There were buttered scones and fruit cake and chocolate biscuits for tea. Leo had orange squash to drink, and Mum and Miss Lyons had tea that smelled like old bonfires. The striped cat sat on Leo's lap again, and Miss Lyons said that his name was Moggy.

"I'm afraid I don't have as much imagination as you," she told Leo. "Isn't it funny how we're all here together this afternoon? There's Moggy the cat, there — and you're Leo, the lion — and I'm Miss Lyons! Isn't that strange?"

And Leo had to agree that it was.

On the first day back at school, Leo and his friend Andrew lined up together in the playground. When the bell rang, they went in together. After they had hung up their coats in the cloakroom, Andrew started to go the old way, to Mrs Ellis's classroom.

"Where are you going?" Leo asked him.

"To class," said Andrew. Then he realized. "Oh," he said. "I forgot. We're not in Mrs Ellis's class any more, are we?"

"No," said Leo. "We're bigger now. We're older. We're in Miss Lyons's class this year."

And off they went, together.

I HATE ROLAND ROBERTS

Martina Selway

ROSIE has started a new school.

She doesn't like it.

She doesn't like being a new girl.

She doesn't like sitting next to a BOY.

And she does not like Roland Roberts!

26a Tower Flats
Molesey
Surrey

Dear Grandad,
I hate my new school. It's very big and strange and I don't know anyone. Miss West the teacher is all right but she made me sit next to a BOY called Roland Roberts! At lunchtime she told him to look after me.
Roland Roberts said, "Girls are stupid." Girls are not stupid and I don't want him to look after me.
I hate Roland Roberts!

At break we all went outside and ran around playing games. Some of the children were so rough that I fell over and knocked my hand. I only cried a bit.

Roland Roberts said, "It didn't hurt you, cry baby."

It DID hurt and I'm not a cry baby. I hate Roland Roberts.

When Mum came to meet me
out of school, she started talking
to Mrs Roberts. She asked her
to come to tea one day soon
so that Roland and I could
play together.

Roland Roberts said, "Yuk!"
I made a horrible face. I'm
not playing with HIM.
I hate Roland Roberts.

I took Annabel to school today.
At playtime some of the boys
ran off with her and threw her
into the tree. Miss West was
very cross and got her down
with an umbrella.

Roland Roberts said, "It wasn't
us, miss."

But I knew it was, horrible
Roland Roberts.

Ugh! Mrs Roberts and Roland came round to tea and I had to take him to my room to play. I got out my toy cars and garage.

Roland Roberts said, "I didn't think soppy girls liked cars, these old ones are brill."

He doesn't know anything, stupid Roland Roberts.

I was very excited this morning
because it had snowed in the night
and everywhere was white all over.
At school everyone was sliding and
throwing snowballs. One hit me right
on my ear.
Roland Roberts said, "Good shot!
Are you all right, Ginge?"
I'm not going to be called Ginge
by silly Roland Roberts.

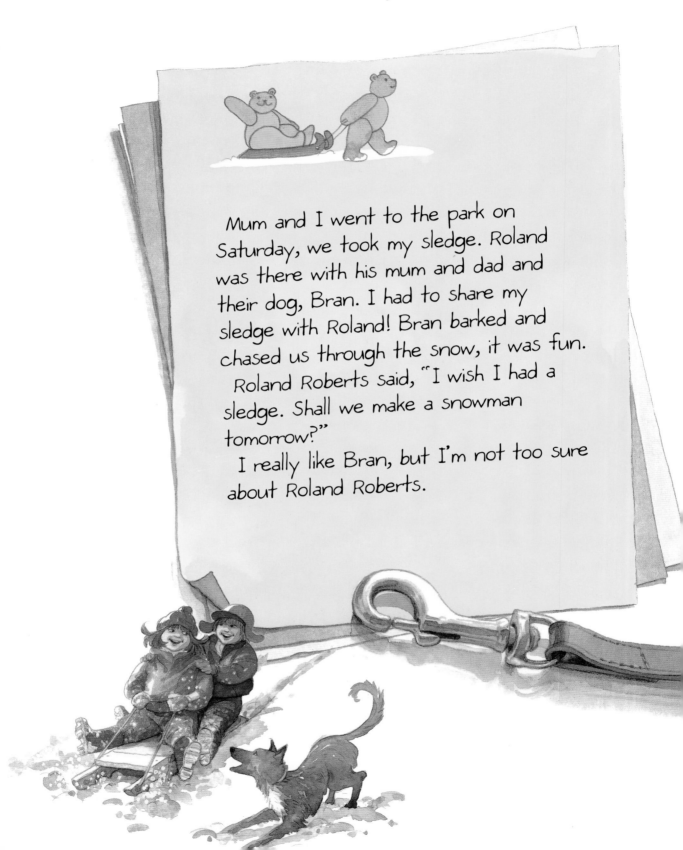

Mum and I went to the park on Saturday, we took my sledge. Roland was there with his mum and dad and their dog, Bran. I had to share my sledge with Roland! Bran barked and chased us through the snow, it was fun.

Roland Roberts said, "I wish I had a sledge. Shall we make a snowman tomorrow?"

I really like Bran, but I'm not too sure about Roland Roberts.

We made the biggest, fattest snowman you ever saw. It was nearly dark when we finished.
I took Mr Roberts's hat and put it on top. He called me a cheeky rascal and pretended to be cross.
Roland Roberts said, "My dad thinks you're the cat's whiskers."
I suppose, he's not so bad, Roland Roberts.

Guess what? Roland's got a pet rat,
his mum lets him keep it in the
kitchen. I had to be very gentle
when I held it because it's
having babies.

Roland Roberts said, "When she has
her babies, you can have one, Ginge."
I've always wanted a pet rat.
He's quite nice, Roland Roberts.

I showed Roland some photos of
me when I stayed on the farm.
He's never been on a farm and didn't
know that pigs could have thirteen
piglets. I told him I was going
to be a farmer when I grow up.

Roland Roberts said, "So am I, that's
what I want to be."

He really likes animals.

I quite like Roland Roberts.

Now we are doing the Christmas
play at school. Miss West said that
if Roland doesn't behave himself
he won't be Joseph.

Roland Roberts said, "I don't want to
be Joseph unless Ginge is Mary."

Can I bring Roland to see you at
the farm soon? He's my best friend.
I like Roland Roberts a LOT!
                Love from
                    Old Ginger Nut. X

Mr J. Lee,
Griggs Farm,
Arklegarthdale,
Yorkshire.

YOU'RE ALL ANIMALS

Nicholas Allan

I WENT to my new school on Monday.

"This is Billy Trunk," said Teacher.
Everyone smiled. But I didn't like them.
They were all different.
There was no one like me.

One had teeth all down his nose . . .

One was slimy . . .

One was spotty . . .

and one smelt really bad.

I wouldn't talk to any of them.

When I got home I told Mum and Dad,
"I want a friend who's just like me."

"I know," said Dad. "Let's see if we can find one on the computer." So Dad typed:

MY NAME'S
BILLY TRUNK.
I'M 7 AND
I LIKE
SKATEBOARDING.

The next day at school I had to do
PE with someone with weird arms.

When I got home Dad turned on the computer.

WATCHA BILLY!
GUESS WHAT? I'M
LIKE YOU. I'M 7,
AND I SKATEBOARD
TOO! FROM FRANK

"Wow! Frank sounds just like me!"
So I typed:

DEAR FRANK,
I LIKE
EATING BUNS!
FROM BILLY

The next day at school I had to sit at lunch with
someone who ate strange food with a dribble-tongue.

I couldn't wait to get home.

"Wow! Frank's just like me!"

So I typed:

The next day at school someone sat down beside me who I thought was really creepy.

When I got home:

WATCHA, BILLY!
ROSEHILL SCHOOL'S
A PLACE I KNOW.
I'LL TELL YOU
WHY, IT'S WHERE
I GO!

So then I typed:

Next morning:

"That Frank is just like me!"

I ran to school. I couldn't wait to meet Frank.
At last I had a friend who was just like me.

When I got there I looked and looked.
I couldn't see Frank anywhere.

But just then I heard a voice call out, "Watcha, Billy!"
I turned, and that's when I saw my great friend Frank,
who I already knew for sure was just like me!

ACKNOWLEDGEMENTS

The publishers gratefully acknowledge the following authors and illustrators:

Leaving Mrs Ellis published by The Bodley Head Children's Books
Text © Catherine Robinson, 1994 Illustrations © Sue Broadley, 1994
These illustrations have been taken from the Bodley Head edition
of *Leaving Mrs Ellis*. While the publishers have made every effort to locate
the owner of the illustrations without success, they would be pleased
to hear from the illustrator or illustrator's estate.

Ruby to the Rescue published by Hutchinson Children's Books
Text and illustrations © Maggie Glen, 1992

Rabbit Gets Ready published by The Bodley Head Children's Books
Text and illustrations © Claire Fletcher, 1995

Unicorn Dreams published by Hutchinson Children's Books
Text © Dyan Sheldon, 1997 Illustrations © Neil Reed, 1997

The Long, Blue Blazer published by Andersen Press Ltd
Text © Jeanne Willis, 1987 Illustrations © Susan Varley, 1987

I Hate Roland Roberts published by Hutchinson Children's Books
Text and illustrations © Martina Selway, 1993

You're All Animals published by Hutchinson Children's Books
Text and illustrations © Nicholas Allan, 2000

Bad Boris Goes to School published by Hutchinson Children's Books
Text and illustrations © Susie Jenkin-Pearce, 1989